For Emmaline

Tucker Pfeffercorn

AN OLD STORY RETOLD

Barry Moser

Little, Brown and Company

Boston New York Toronto London

One cold Sunday morning, a bunch of miners were swapping stories down at Sweatt's Company Store. George Biggers had just capped Wallis Swinney with a tale about being out 'possum hunting one night and coming across a knot of witches dancing around a fire. Well, not to be outdone, Jefferson Tadlock began inventing the wildest and most outrageous story anybody thereabouts had ever heard. To make it more believable, he used the names of people they all knew, like Jack Blaylock the moonshiner, and Haskel Birdsong the hobo, and old Marlon Tubbs and his three-legged pig. It was so funny, the miners were all laughing and hooting and slapping their knees. And when he had convinced every last one of them that it was all true, Tadlock finished his crazy tale with a bit about a woman who could spin cotton into gold.

"Who's the woman, Tadlock?" Wade Ellison asked.

"That little ol' widow-woman up on the hill," Jefferson Tadlock replied.

"Bessie Grace Kinzalow?" asked Wallis Swinney.

"Yep," Jefferson Tadlock said. "I seen her do it."

"My hind foot!" a surly voice said.

Jefferson Tadlock turned around, saying, "No, really, she can," but when he saw who he was speaking to, he went weak in the knees and funny in the stomach. It was Hezakiah Sweatt, the meanest man in the mountains. The richest, too. He owned *everything* for miles around — the mines, the cotton fields, the company store, and the houses the miners lived in. He overpriced everything in the company store and threw families out in the cold if their rent was even one day late. Worst of all, rumor had it that he had had Sam Whitlock and Windon Armfield killed because they crossed him.

Hezakiah Sweatt stared at Jefferson Tadlock. A drool of brown tobacco juice leached out of the corner of his mouth as he said again, "My hind foot."

Too scared to retreat from his story, Jefferson Tadlock said, "She really can, Mr. Sweatt. I swear. I seen her."

Greed burned in Hezakiah Sweatt's eyes. "You better be right, you slack-twisted sand-lapper. Go git her so's I can see for myself."

Bessie Grace Kinzalow was nineteen years old. Her husband, Donny Bruce, had died in the mines just the year before — an "accident," according to Hezakiah Sweatt. They had a little daughter, Claretta, who she carried everywhere with her, even to Hezakiah Sweatt's cotton fields, where Bessie Grace hoed cotton every day but Sunday — hard work, especially if Hezakiah Sweatt was around. But Bessie Grace worked happily because Claretta was always with her, usually asleep in a little basket covered with an umbrella. Bessie Grace was fearless and strong willed, and when Jefferson Tadlock came and told her about what he had done down at Sweatt's store, Bessie Grace said, "Jefferson Tadlock, don't you know how much trouble your tales cause? Now I have to go down there and straighten all this out." Then she packed up Claretta, put on her coat, and walked down to the company store. Jefferson Tadlock tagged behind. When she got there, she went straight up to Hezakiah Sweatt and said, "Mr. Sweatt, I don't know what's going on here, but you and everybody else knows what kind of liar Jefferson Tadlock is and I tell you honestly, sir, I can't do this thing he said I can."

Hezakiah Sweatt grabbed Bessie Grace by the arm and growled, "Let's us just see."

Bessie Grace tried to free herself, but Hezakiah Sweatt squeezed tighter, then pulled her and Claretta out through the back door and down into an old shed. One of his thugs, Burley Ray Liles, followed.

The shed was a shambles, strewn with hay and littered with washtubs, flour sacks, a couple of old spinning wheels, and a half bale of cotton.

Hezakiah Sweatt pushed Bessie Grace and Claretta inside and stood by the door, unlocking a big padlock. "This oughta do pretty good, gal," he said. "Whaddya think?" Bessie Grace looked him straight in the eye, smiled, and kicked him in the shin as hard as she could. Then she bolted for the door, but Hezakiah Sweatt snatched Claretta away and handed her to Burley Ray Liles. Bessie Grace made a wild effort to get Claretta back, but Hezakiah Sweatt thrust his hairy nose into her face and said, "If'n ya want yore baby back, ya best get to work, cause if'n that there cotton ain't gold by mornin'"— he paused —"why, I'd just hate to think what might happen to yore sweet little ol' baby." Then he locked the door.

Word of the incident spread quickly. Everybody wanted to go help Bessie Grace, but nobody did because they were all afraid they might end up like Sam Whitlock or Windon Armfield.

And so Bessie Grace stayed locked up in Hezakiah Sweatt's shed. She paced and fretted about Claretta and tried to figure out how to escape. By nightfall her worry and exasperation had worn her out, so she lay down and stared up into the dark ceiling. That was when she noticed a small pair of feet dangling from the rafters.

When she stood to see better, a peculiar little man bounded to the floor.

Bessie Grace yelped, *"Lord o' mercy!* Who are you?"

"Looks to me like ya got a bit o' trouble, Missy," the peculiar little man said. "Anything I can he'p ya with?"

Bessie Grace said, "That nasty old Hezakiah Sweatt locked me up in here, stole my baby, and is of the opinion that I can spin this cotton here into gold, which of course I can't do any more than a man in the moon."

"Hey, I can he'p ya do that," said the peculiar little man. Then he set the spinning wheel spinning and spinning into a bright blurrrrr. In a minute, lo and behold, he had spun out three skeins of gold thread.

"Why, I swan," said Bessie Grace. "How did you do that?"

"It ain't nothin 'tall," the peculiar little man replied.

"I don't know how to thank you," Bessie Grace said. "Can I give you something?"

"I don't want nothin'," he said in a sweet voice. "Not now, no-how." Then without another word, he raised his foot over his head, slammed it to the floor, and disappeared in a billow of dust, hay, and motes of cotton lint.

The next morning, Hezakiah Sweatt arrived just as the sun came up. He unlocked the padlock, threw the door open, and startled Bessie Grace from her sleep. When she saw who it was, she yelled at him, "What have you done with Claretta, you nasty old man! Give me my baby back!"

Hezakiah Sweatt ignored her and picked up the gold. "Why, gal, it looks like ya done a purty good job here," he said.

"Well, let me go then," said Bessie Grace.

"Could," Hezakiah Sweatt said, "but Burley Ray done brung ya a little more work."

So Hezakiah Sweatt locked Bessie Grace up again, this time with five bales of cotton. Her only hope was that her peculiar little friend would come again.

And he did. Just like the night before, he jumped down from the rafters.

"I wish you wouldn't do that!" Bessie Grace said. "It nearly scares me to death! How long have you been up there, anyway?"

"Looks to me like ya got a whole heap more trouble tonight than ya did last night, Miss Bessie Grace," the peculiar little man said.

And before she even asked for his help, he set into motion a spectacle of light and cotton . . . and gold. *Whirrr. Whrrrr. Whrrrrr.*

When he had finished and the skeins of gold thread were draped neatly beside the spinning wheel, a grateful and astonished Bessie Grace asked the peculiar little man once again, "Isn't there something I can give you?"

"Naw . . . ," he said, "but maybe one of these days I'll take me som'thin'." And with that, the peculiar little man stomped his foot and disappeared in a sneeze of hay and dust and lint.

At daybreak, Hezakiah Sweatt burst in to collect his prize — thirty skeins of gold thread!

Bessie Grace, realizing what she was up against, simply asked, "Mr. Sweatt, can I please see Claretta? Can I take her home now?"

"Stop whining and listen," Hezakiah Sweatt said. "I gotta go over to Belle Spring on bizness. The boys brung ya some vittles and a little more work to do while I'm gone. After I get back, we might just have to get ya a bigger place to work."

And Hezakiah Sweatt locked up Bessie Grace once again — this time with twelve bales of cotton, some cold bacon, a skillet of cornbread, a pitcher of buttermilk, and scarcely enough room to turn around in.

That night the peculiar little man once again appeared. "I can't tell you how happy I am to see you!" Bessie Grace said.

"Ol' Sweatt makes it hard for ya, don't he?" said the peculiar little man.

"I hate to ask," Bessie Grace began, "you've been so good to me already, but can you help me again . . . and . . . could you maybe help me get out of here? I'll give you anything I've got."

"Ya got a deal." Soon a blizzard of light and cotton and gold filled the air just as it had the nights before. And then it was all over. The cotton was gone, the burlap wrappings lay empty on the floor, and a fine dusting of white lint covered everything except the newly spun seventy-two skeins of gold.

The peculiar little man said, "See ya later," and with a stomp, he was gone.

Bessie Grace fell asleep wondering if she would ever escape.

Hezakiah Sweatt never came back. Some said he was done in by a bunch of miners over at his Belle Spring mine. Others said he was eaten by bears. Nobody knew for sure. But what did happen for sure was this: when the news came early in the morning, it caused such a ruckus Bessie Grace woke up. She peeked through a crack and saw Burley Ray Liles running toward the company store. Then she noticed that the door of the shed was standing ajar and that the padlock was lying in the hay next to where she had been sleeping. She scrambled about, gathering up the gold skeins into one of the burlap wrappers. She slung the sack over her shoulder, grabbed up the iron skillet, and stormed out of the shed and through the back door of Sweatt's store. She found Claretta safe and sound in the back room. She whisked her up in her arms, and without saying a single word to any of the astonished people gathered there, she marched out through the screen doors and onto the front porch. And there stood Sweatt's thugs! Well, without a moment's hesitation, Bessie Grace went right up to Burley Ray Liles and told him that if he tried to stop her, she'd brain him with the skillet. Then with a proud and sassy toss of her head, Bessie Grace headed home.

One night later on, while Bessie Grace was sitting reading her Bible, she heard Claretta start to cry. When she went to check on her, there, standing beside the crib, was the peculiar little man.

"Hey!" Bessie Grace said. "I've been wondering when you'd drop by."

"I come to get what ya owe me," he said. His voice was suddenly fiendish and jolted Bessie Grace with fear.

"It's in the other room," she said.

"Now, you listen to me, gal," said the nasty little man. "*I* took care of ol' Hezakiah Sweatt fer ya, an' *I* turned ya loose from that shed. *Me!*" he shouted. "*Me!*" He jumped onto a chair and thrust his face up close to hers. She smelled his moldy breath as he said, "And now ya're gonna give me *anything* I want, jus' like you said you'uz a-gonna do."

"What do you want?" asked Bessie Grace.

"The chile, honey, the *chile.*"

"Claretta? You want Claretta?"

"Ya said *anything*, an' the anything I want is *her!*"

"Well, I don't care — you can't have her!"

"Oh, yes, I can . . . else somethin' awful might happen to her."

Bessie Grace protested. She argued. She pleaded. She begged. Finally the nasty little man put his hands over his ears and said, "ALL RIGHT, ALL RIGHT — I tell ya what. We'll play us a little game. Win, an' I'll forget that ya owe me. Lose, an' I get the chile."

"What kind of game?" Bessie Grace asked.

"Guessin' game."

"Guessing what?"

"My name."

"I have to guess your name? Now?"

"Naw. I'll come back day after tomorrow. I'll even give ya three guesses to come up with it . . . but then I'm a-taking the baby."

Then he gave out one big *stomp* and disappeared.

Bessie Grace lay awake that night, trying every name she could think of. Names like Alvester and Arnell and Bryce and Burdette and Cheevers and Clermon and Darden and Dewitt and Eckford and Erlbee and Fulton and Faison, but she never came up with a name that seemed like it could belong to that nasty little man. So the next day she took Claretta and headed off in search of the name.

They walked and searched all morning and all afternoon, but she found no name. Evening came, and still nothing. Then just as she was about to give up and turn back toward home, Bessie Grace saw a pale light off in a roadside cemetery. Lightning bugs, she thought, but then she noticed it didn't blink. Curious, she gently shushed Claretta and crept toward the light. And there among the headstones she saw the nasty little man, dancing and singing:

> *Wheel & spin! Wheel & spin!*
> *She'll loose a chile, and I will win!*
> *My name from me ain't never been torn!*
> *It's Tucker! Tucker Pfeffercorn!*

She had it! She had his name! She crept away, hugging Claretta to her shoulder and saying over and over to herself, "Tucker Pfeffercorn, Tucker Pfeffercorn, Tucker Pfeffercorn . . ." And when she was safely away, she ran as fast as she could.

The nasty little man appeared the next night just before Claretta's bedtime. At first Bessie Grace pretended not to notice him and continued about her chores, peeling crab apples for a cobbler she was making.

Casually she said, "Well, we've been expecting you."

"Ready to play our little game?" said the nasty little man as he poked at Bessie Grace with his cane.

"Three guesses, right?" Bessie Grace asked, not looking at him.

"Right."

"And if I get it right, you'll go away and leave us alone?"

"Yep. Won't bother ya no more. But don't worry — you ain't gonna get it."

Bessie Grace stood up and began to pace around the kitchen, pretending to think.

"Well, let's see. How about . . . Stanley Stinkbreath?"

"No. That ain't it," the nasty little man said with a chuckle.

"Well, how about . . . Buddy Boogernose?"

"Nope . . . but them's pretty good guesses."

Then after a long pause, she said, "Hmmm, let's see. . . . How about . . . how about *Tucker Pfeffercorn?*"

Well, when he heard his name, it enraged the nasty little man so much that he stomped and stomped around the room. He bounced up to the ceiling and hung upside down, screaming, "The devil told ya! The devil told ya!" He bounded to the floor, screaming, "Ya ain't gonna git away with it! Ya ain't gonna git away with it!" Then he started in stomping again. He stomped outside, and he stomped and screamed, and stomped and screamed, and stomped some more. And then he stomped one time too many, and his foot got stuck. He pulled and pulled on that stuck foot, mumbling, "TuckerTuckerTuckerTuckerTucker." He huffed and pulled, and huffed and pulled . . . and then just as he screamed out, "TUCKER PFEFFERCORN!" *pfuff!* The air filled with a musty billow of yellow and green dust. Tucker Pfeffercorn had split himself in two!

Things went pretty well for Bessie Grace after that. She gave a good bit of the gold to her church, but most of it she kept. A few months later, she and Claretta moved to Cincinnati, where they lived happily ever after.

First Edition

Library of Congress Cataloging-in-Publication Data

Moser, Barry.
    Tucker Pfeffercorn : An old story retold / Barry Moser. — 1st ed.
        p.   cm.
    Summary: A retelling of the classic Rumpelstiltskin tale with a Southern setting.
    ISBN 0-316-58542-4
    [1. Fairy tales.   2. Folklore — Germany.]   I. Title.
PZ8.M8464Tu   1994
398.2 — dc20
[E]   92-34340

SC   10   9   8   7   6   5   4   3   2   1

Published simultaneously in Canada
by Little, Brown & Company (Canada) Limited

Paintings done in watercolor on paper handmade at the Barcham Green Paper Mills, Maidstone, G.B., in 1983.
Color separations made by Universal Colour Scanning Ltd. Text set in Monotype Bell by The Sarabande Press. Hand lettering done by Reassurance Wunder.

Printed and bound by South China Printing
Printed in Hong Kong

The author wishes to thank Paul Mariani for Tucker's song; Lt. Roland LaCasse, Massachusetts State Police, Emily MacLachlan, and Izzy Harper for their wonderful faces; Frank White, Laurie Smith, and Joanne Williamson at Old Sturbridge Village for their expertise on spinning; and Jane Dyer and Patricia MacLachlan for their friendship and support.